Angel and Me
and the
Bayside Bombers

Angel and Me
and the
Bayside Bombers

by Mary Jane Auch

Illustrated by Cat Bowman Smith

Little, Brown and Company

Boston   Toronto   London

Text copyright © 1989 by Mary Jane Auch
Illustrations copyright © 1989 by Cat Bowman Smith

First Edition

Springboard Books and design is a trademark of Little, Brown
and Company (Inc.)

Library of Congress Cataloging-in-Publication Data

Auch, Mary Jane.
    Angel and me and the Bayside bombers/by Mary Jane Auch;
illustrated by Cat Bowman Smith.
        p.   cm.
    Summary: Having been kicked off the third-grade soccer
team, Brian challenges them to a match against his own team,
a team which he and his cousin Angel hasten to create and
whip into shape — if possible.
    ISBN 0-316-05914-5
    [1. Soccer — Fiction.]   I. Smith, Cat Bowman, ill.
II. Title.
PZ7.A898An   1989   89–31646
[E] — dc 19   CIP
                                                AC

10 9 8 7 6 5 4 3 2 1

WOR

Published simultaneously in Canada
by Little, Brown & Company (Canada) Limited

Printed in the United States of America

For Ian and Jeff,
with thanks for their soccer tips

1

On the first nice Saturday in June, every other kid in the third grade was outside doing something great. Not me. I was stuffed in the backseat of our car between my two older sisters, on the way to Cousin Emily's wedding.

"I never even heard of Cousin Emily," I said. "How come I never laid eyes on her in my whole life? They only live twenty minutes away from us."

Mom glanced over her shoulder. "Don't be silly, Brian. Of course you remember your cousin. We have pictures of you and Emily having pony rides at Seneca Park."

"That was me and Kate, Mom," my sister LeeAnn said. "Brian wasn't even born yet when you and Aunt Vivian had the big fight."

"It was not a fight, LeeAnn," Mom said. "We simply had a disagreement over . . . isn't that funny? I can't even remember what it was."

My sister Kate leaned forward. "I remember, Mom. Aunt Vivian called you a dumb, stupid, dim-witted . . ."

Mom whipped her head around so fast her dangly earring smacked her right in the nose. "That's enough, Kate! We're going to forget the past. We're going to have a lovely . . . Brian, what on earth are you wearing?"

"Clothes," I said.

"Why didn't you wear your good suit?"

"You didn't say you wanted me to wear my good suit."

"Why do you think I had it laid out on your bed?"

"I thought you were just airing it out."

"Brian Hegney," Mom said, "what are the relatives going to think when you arrive at a wedding wearing jeans and a T-shirt?"

Kate snorted. "They'll think he's a dumb, stupid, dim-witted . . ."

"All right, knock it off," Dad said.

That shut everybody up. Dad never said much, but when he told you to knock it off, he meant it.

We passed a field where a bunch of kids were playing soccer. That's where I should have been — practicing my brains out. If I could prove to Steve Grebe that I was a dynamite player, maybe he'd let me be on the neighborhood soccer team, the Bayside Bombers.

Steve only let the best players on the Bombers, not that anybody had put him in charge. When you're as big as Steve Grebe, you get to be in charge automatically. Besides, he owned the soccer ball.

"Here's the sign for Scottsville," Dad said. "What church are we looking for?"

Mom dug through her purse. "I must have left the invitation at home. It was Saint something-or-other."

LeeAnn rolled her eyes. "Well, that narrows it down."

Dad slowed as we approached a church. "The sign says Saint John's," Kate said. "Is that it?"

Mom bit her lip. "That doesn't ring a bell. I think it started with an *S*. Keep going."

We spent the next twenty minutes zeroing in on steeples. We found the United Methodist, the First Baptist, and radio station KZIX. We didn't find a saint that began with an *S*.

Just as Dad was about to turn around and go home, Mom yelled, "There it is — Saint Cecelia's!"

Mom was the only one in the family who spelled worse than me.

2

When we got inside the church, I ended up in the aisle seat. At least I'd get a good view of the action.

Some lady dressed in purple sang in a warbly voice. Dad started snoring until Mom poked him.

Then two guys unrolled a white cloth down the aisle. That seemed dumb. If they wanted to keep the rug clean, they should have covered it up before all the people came in.

The organ started playing "Here comes the bride, big, fat, and wide," and two kids came down the aisle. There was a girl with a basket of flowers and a boy carrying a pillow. I guess he thought he was going to have trouble staying awake, like Dad.

Some ladies in pink dresses came next. They walked funny, like they weren't in any hurry to get to the front of the church. Then the bride came in, and everybody stood up.

"I can't believe Emily turned out so well," Mom whispered as the bride went by. "She was such a homely child."

The lady in front of us turned and gave Mom a dirty look.

The wedding went on for a long time. There was a lot of standing up and sitting down. Then the purple warbler sang another song.

Finally it was over, and we went to the reception. The place was mobbed. Mom pushed through the crowd and headed for a short fat lady. They hugged each other and starting crying.

"What's wrong with Mom?" I asked.

"Don't worry," Kate said. "She and Aunt Vivian are just making up."

Mom motioned for us to come over. "Is that my little LeeAnn and Kate, all grown up?" Aunt Vivian cooed, giving them each a big hug. I tried to hide behind Mom, but Aunt Vivian spotted me. "And who's this?"

Mom pulled me in front of her. "Brian, our youngest."

"I never knew you had a son, Mildred," Aunt Vivian squealed. "What a cutie." She pinched my cheeks with both hands and gave them a shake. I was sure she had killed my smile muscles.

I tried to get away, but she grabbed my hand. "I'm going to take this new man in the family and introduce him to all his aunts and uncles and cousins. What do you think about that, Brian?" Before I could say anything, she gave me a one-handed cheek pinch.

We took off across the room. "This is your Uncle Lou, Aunt Marie, and Aunt Christine. Brian is Mildred's boy. Isn't he a sweetheart?"

Aunt Marie and Aunt Christine each gave me a double cheek pinch. What was this, the family handshake?

"This is your cousin Angel, Brian," Aunt Vivian said. She shoved me into a chair next to a skinny girl with daisies in her frizzy blond hair. "She's just your age. You two can get to know each other."

Aunt Vivian was about to lay a double cheek pinch on Angel. Just then, Angel blew a huge bubble. Aunt Vivian changed her mind and left us alone.

Angel stared at me, cracking her gum. "What happened to your face? Your cheeks are all red and puffy."

"Everybody here pinches," I said.

Angel grinned, showing the gap where her

front teeth should be. "You gotta have bubble gum. That's the only thing that stops 'em." She pulled a pink wad out of her mouth. "You want to borrow mine for a while? It's broken in."

"No, thanks. I'll just duck from now on."

She popped the gum back into her mouth and shrugged. "It's *your* face."

Angel and I couldn't think of anything else to say, so we just watched the adults do stupid things. Cousin Emily and the groom cut the cake. Then they mashed big pieces of it into each other's faces. If I ever did that, I'd be grounded for a week.

Then the groom reached up under Cousin Emily's skirt and pulled this lace rubber band off her leg. I almost dropped my teeth! He threw it to some guys. Cousin Emily got so mad, she threw her flowers at a whole bunch of ladies. I thought there was going to be a good fight, but then the band started playing. Emily and the groom began dancing, like

nothing had happened. Grown-ups are weird.

"Come on," Angel said. "Let's get some cake."

As I followed her, I almost bumped into a kid who was carrying a huge plate of cake and ice cream. He was dressed like a real nerd — shiny black shoes, pink knee socks, and short pants. He had a pink shirt with ruffles all over it and . . . a very familiar face. It was Steve Grebe, captain of the Bayside Bombers.

I gave him a big smile. "Hi, Steve," I said. "Nice outfit . . . especially the pink ruffles."

When he recognized me, his face turned bright red, which clashed with his shirt. As we looked each other in the eye, Steve Grebe and I both knew I'd be playing on the Bayside Bombers from now on.

3

I could hardly wait for lunch at school. That was the only time I ever saw Steve Grebe, because he was in one of the other third-grade sections. I spotted him in the cafeteria with a bunch of the Bombers.

"Hi, Steve," I said. "What time is the game after school?"

Jessie Jablonski, the only girl on the team, blew her straw paper at me. "What's it to you, nerd? You want to watch?"

"No, I'm playing."

"Playing what, dolls?" Jessie said. Everybody laughed, including Steve.

I stood my ground. "No, soccer. Steve said I could. Right, Steve?"

Moose Murphy, one of the biggest Bombers, looked at Steve. "What are you, crazy? You never said that, did you?"

Steve didn't answer. He pretended to be real interested in what was in his lunchbox.

"Did you?" Jessie asked.

Steve peeked inside his sandwich. "Did I what?"

"Did you say the pipsqueak here could be on the Bombers?" Moose asked. The others leaned forward to hear Steve's answer.

Steve looked at the table of angry faces. "Naw, I never said he could be on the team."

"Sure you did." I picked up a napkin from the table. "You remember. It was Saturday?" I was folding the napkin back and forth as I talked. "We were out in Scottsville?" I held the folded napkin up to my throat. It looked

just like the ruffles on Steve's pink wedding shirt.

It took Steve a second or two to make the connection. Then his face got red. He knocked the napkin out of my hand. "Yeah, all of a sudden I remember."

"Remember what?" Jessie asked, standing up so fast she tipped over her milk carton.

Steve jumped up to get out of the way of the milk. "I told him he could play."

Steve and Jessie stood glaring at each other as a pool of milk spread over the table. Jessie's eyes narrowed to little slits. "He'd better be good."

Steve didn't even notice the milk dripping on his sneaker as he stood there with his fists clenched. "Yeah," he said, turning to look at me. "He'd better be good."

4

I never sat through such a long school day in my whole life. For a while, I'd be so excited about the game I could hardly sit still. Then I'd remember the Bombers' faces, and I wanted to back out. I finally decided everything would be okay after they saw me play. After all, I'd been practicing in my backyard for weeks.

I was grabbing a snack for energy when Mom came into the kitchen. "Do you remember meeting your cousin Angel from Indiana at Emily's wedding?" she asked.

"No, I don't think so, Mom."

"I'm sure you did, Brian. You were sitting at the table with her for the longest time."

"Oh, her," I said, gulping down a glass of milk. "I didn't know where she was from."

"Well, her parents went back home, and she's staying with Vivian for the rest of the month."

"How come she's not in school?"

"Their schools are on a different schedule from ours. This is her summer vacation."

"Oh. I gotta go, Mom. I'm late."

Mom grabbed my arm. "Don't you think it would be nice to invite her over sometime?"

"Yeah, sure," I said, just so she'd let go of me. "See you."

The team was already warming up when I got there.

"Okay," Steve yelled. "Everybody get over here so I can assign positions."

I did a couple of my cool moves on the way over to Steve, pretending I was dribbling a ball, dodging big guys. I would've looked really good, if I hadn't tripped over my shoelace.

Steve looked down at me as I sprawled at his feet. "Not you, stupid. You're on the bench."

"What bench?" I asked, looking around.

"He just means you don't play," Moose said. "Sit over there on the ground until we need you."

"Which will be never," Jessie added.

I went over to the edge of the field and sat under a tree. The kids from the Kingston Trailer Park team were on the other side of the field. I knew them all from school, but they looked bigger now — and meaner.

Steve was arguing with Ben Weston, the captain of the Kingston Killers. "If Wally isn't here by now, you'll have to start without him," Ben said. "Call in your sub."

Steve started over toward me, but Jessie stopped him. "We're better off playing a man short," she said. "The nerd can't even run across the field without breaking his neck. The Killers are tough. We can't afford any mistakes."

"They won't let us play a man short," Steve said. "We'd have to forfeit. Brian, you're left wing."

With all the practicing I'd done in my back-yard, I'd never learned what the positions were called in soccer. When you just play by yourself, it doesn't matter. I tried to fake it. I figured they weren't so wild about having me play, so they probably wanted me in the back.

"Where do you think you're going?" Steve shouted. "I said left *wing*."

Wing? What was I supposed to do, run with my arms out to the sides? I could see there was a lot about soccer I didn't know.

Jessie was in the center of the front line. "Up here, nerd," she yelled. "Move it, so we can start."

I slipped into the empty space next to Jessie, then looked at the other team. There were ten faces who looked as if they were ready to murder me. No wonder they were called the Killers.

5

Playing a real game of soccer was nothing like practicing in my backyard. For the first ten minutes, I couldn't keep track of the ball. Every time I saw a bunch of kids kicking each other, I'd run over. By the time I got there, the ball would be sailing down to the other end of the field. Once the ball came right at me. I wound up for a big kick, but I never even nicked it. Jessie shoved me out of the way and charged toward the goal with the ball. Then one of the Killers got it away from her. He dribbled it all the way down the field, and Steve blocked it in our goal.

Soon I got pretty tired running back and forth. I was off to one side, resting, when the ball rolled toward me.

"Go, Brian," somebody yelled. I took off, dribbling like crazy. I made it around the first two Killers, but when I got to the third one, I zigged when I should have zagged. He plowed through me like I was made of cardboard.

Somebody behind me said, "Nice try."

Wow! I couldn't believe it. I was really playing soccer — on a real team. I was a Bayside Bomber!

All the action was by the Killers' goal, so I ran back there. I was just thinking about how great it was to be on the Bombers, when something smashed me right between the eyes and knocked me over. It was the ball. The Killers' goalie caught it as it bounced off my head. He kicked it way back down the field.

"You just blocked my goal, nerd," Jessie shouted. "That would've been our point for sure."

A buzzer went off. Jessie had brought the timer from her mother's stove to time the halves. Both teams went to their sidelines. The other Bombers were glaring at me as they got drinks from the water jug. "If your head gets in my way again," Jessie said, "I'll take it clean off."

During the second half, I tried to stay away from the ball. I figured I'd get in less trouble that way. If I went home and practiced real hard after the game, I'd be better next time.

The game was almost over when the ball landed right at my feet. I didn't even have to stop it.

Somebody yelled, "Go for it!" and I took

off. As I charged down the field, I dodged around player after player. Nobody even tried to stop me. It was just like being in the backyard, except for all the yelling. When I got to the end of the field, I slipped that ball into the goal. I slipped it right past the hands of . . . Steve Grebe!

"What are you doing in the Killers' goal?" I whispered.

Steve glared at me. "This is *our* goal, you nerd! We switched goals between halves."

Just then the timer went off and Ben came running over. "We win! One to nothing!" he shouted. "Thanks to you, Brian." He pounded me on the back.

Jessie stood nose to nose with Steve. "You throw Brian off the team right now, or I'm leaving. It's him or me."

"That goes for me, too," Moose said. Pretty soon everybody on the whole team was crowding around, threatening to quit.

"Well?" Jessie said. "Is it him or us?"

"I can't just kick him off the team," Steve said. "It has to be a vote. All in favor of Brian not being on the team, raise your hands."

I didn't stay around to see the vote. I knew how it was going to turn out.

6

Mom was in my bedroom when I got home. "Brian, I have a wonderful surprise for you. You have to clean your room."

"Some surprise, Mom. What do I get after that? A trip to the dentist?"

"Don't get smart with me, young man. The surprise is your cousin Angel. She's lonesome at Vivian's, so I invited her to spend the rest of the month here with you."

"Aw, Mom! I don't want a girl hanging

around me. Let LeeAnn or Kate get stuck with her."

"She's exactly your age, Brian. You have lots in common."

"Yeah, like we both have to breathe to stay alive. We should be able to talk about that for hours."

Mom dug under my bed and pulled out a bowl of cereal that had turned into green fur.

"What's this?"

"New kind of cereal," I said. "Fuzzy-O's."

"I'm not sticking my hand under there again," Mom said, getting up. "Get this room cleaned out, so I can make up the bed for Angel."

"Where am I supposed to sleep?"

"Your father set up the tent in the backyard."

"The tent? You're kicking me out of my room to sleep in the tent?"

"You used to beg us to let you sleep out back in a tent."

"That's when I was just a kid," I grumbled. "I was stupid then."

Mom started to pick up the dried-up bat on my desk then changed her mind.

"Be careful," I said, rescuing it from her. "That bat could be a hundred years old. What are you doing with all my stuff, anyway?"

"I'm just going to get it out of sight while Angel is here. I'm sure she doesn't want to sleep in the same room with a hundred-year-old bat."

"Maybe the bat doesn't want to sleep in the same room with a dumb girl."

Mom glared at me. "I want you to make Angel feel at home, Brian. Now that this family is finally back together, we're going to stay that way."

Aunt Vivian brought Angel over after supper. She was even weirder than I'd remembered. Her frizzy hair stuck out in little clumps like a bird's nest.

Mom handed me a suitcase. "Take Angel upstairs to her room, Brian."

"You mean *my* room," I grumbled. I led Angel up the stairs. "Here," I said, opening the door so hard the door knob smashed against the wall. I dumped her suitcase on the floor.

"Where are you sleeping?" Angel asked.

I pointed to the back window. "Out there. In a tent."

"No kidding?" Angel said. "I wish I had a tent."

"Well, I think that could be arranged . . ."

I tried, but Mom didn't go for the idea. "I wouldn't dream of making our guest sleep in the backyard, Brian."

"Oh, sure," I said, "but you'd let your own son — *your own flesh and blood* — sleep outside in a blizzard."

"Chances of a blizzard in June are slim," Mom said, shoving me out the back door.

"Maybe *I* should go stay with Aunt Vivian," I yelled, as the door slammed behind me.

I hung my bat from the tent pole and swung the flashlight beam back and forth. Creepy bat-wing shadows moved across the top of the tent. If Angel was watching out the window, she was probably scared to death.

I checked the window, but the light was out. I knew she was spying on me anyway, so I threw in a few moans and cackles with the moving shadows. That ought to get her.

I kept it up for quite a while, but I didn't hear any screams coming from my room. Maybe Angel had fainted. I climbed into my sleeping bag and turned off the flashlight.

The streetlight threw shadows of leaves and branches across the top of the tent. I was looking up at the bat, when all of a sudden I thought I saw one wing move. Then I could hear breathing. I was pretty sure I smelled bat breath.

I burrowed down in my sleeping bag, trying to forget about the bat. After all, it had been dead a hundred years, right? But what if it was a vampire bat?

Now I was being stupid. Mom wouldn't let me keep a vampire bat in my room . . . right?

I peeked out of my bag. I could see little red eyes glowing in the bat's head. I grabbed the flashlight and turned it on. The bat looked dead again, but I wasn't taking any chances. I took the bat out in the yard and buried it next to Mom's compost heap.

But if it was a vampire bat, it could dig its way out of there. What did they use to kill a vampire in the movies? A stake! I had to drive a wooden stake through the bat's heart.

I ran back and pulled up one of the tent stakes. One side of the tent fell down, but it didn't matter. I had to kill this thing before it got me.

I figured the bat must be pretty mad by now, so I didn't dig it up. I just stuck the stake in the ground over the spot where the bat's heart should be. Then I pounded it in with the shovel.

It was hard getting back into my sleeping bag, because half of the tent was on my head. At least I was safe, now. Unless . . . the stake had missed the bat's heart . . .

With my ear to the ground, I thought I heard something digging. The bat was coming to get me.

I didn't care anymore about being kicked off the Bombers. I didn't even care that my mother had kicked me out of my room. They'd all be sorry in the morning, when they found me with two little bite marks in my neck — the sign of the vampire bat.

7

I must have drifted off to sleep, because I woke up to a steady *thwack-thwack* sound. The sound of bat wings beating on the side of the tent! I opened my eyes, but something was pushing down on my face, smothering me! I let out one last bloodcurdling scream.

Something clutched at my shoulder. "Brian, wake up. You're knocking down your tent."

It was Angel. She was kneeling in the only

corner of the tent that was still up, watching me.

"Did you see it?" I yelled, scrambling out of my sleeping bag.

"See what?"

"The bat. I think it got me. Check my neck." I lifted my chin so she could see the red spots.

"It looks like a regular neck."

I blinked in the bright light and realized it was sunshine. I must have made it through the night. I crawled out of the tent and ran to the compost pile. The stake was still there, pounded into a patch of freshly dug dirt. Suddenly I heard the *thwack-thwack* coming close behind me. I whirled around, ready to face my doom.

It was Angel again. She was dribbling a soccer ball across the yard. It hadn't been bat wings after all.

I tried to look cool, so she wouldn't know

how scared I'd been. "You didn't tell me you played soccer."

Angel stood on one foot, balancing the ball on her other toe. "You never asked."

"You're pretty good. You play on a team?"

"Yep." She dribbled the ball back across the yard. "I'm center striker."

Whatever that was, it sounded important.

"You play?" she asked, as she came back toward me.

"Some." I was going to go after the ball, but I noticed I was in my bare feet. Then I noticed I was also in my pajamas. I made a dive for the tent and pulled the flap closed behind me.

"Now what's wrong?" Angel called through the canvas.

"Nothing. Some people around here have to get ready for school, that's all."

"Well, excuse me for living!" I could hear her dribbling the ball toward the house. I

didn't change into my clothes until I heard the door slam.

It was a miserable day in school. The Bombers were still mad at me. I must have been called a nerd about fifty times. Then the Killers kept thanking me for helping them win. By lunchtime I had just about had it. That's when I made the stupid move.

I was passing the Bombers' table to get to the milk line, when a foot stuck out and tripped me. I looked up into Steve Grebe's grinning face. "Whatsa matter, nerd? Trip over your shoelaces?"

I should have just ignored him and kept walking. But I didn't. "You guys think you're so smart," I yelled. "You think just because you're big and mean you can play soccer better than anyone else. If I had my own team, we could beat the Bombers any day."

Steve's eyes lit up. "So get a team, nerd. The Bombers challenge you to a soccer game Saturday afternoon."

"Yeah," Jessie said, grinning. "And the losers have to buy double-scoop ice cream cones for everybody on the winning team. I want Chocolate Mint Chip."

Before I knew what was happening, Steve shook my hand and sealed the deal right in front of everybody in the whole cafeteria. I was trapped.

I ran all the way home. Angel was my only hope. She was sitting on the back steps with her chin in her hands when I got there.

"Angel, you have to help me," I said. I told her what had happened.

"That was really stupid, Brian. How could you challenge the Bombers? You don't even have a team."

"It's too late to worry about how stupid it was. You said you play on a team. Could you get them to come here for one game?"

"From Indiana? You know how much the bus fare would cost?"

"A lot?"

Angel nodded. "Enough for about a million double-scoop ice cream cones, I bet."

I slumped down on the steps next to her. "I'll never be able to show my face in school again after Saturday."

"You mean you're just giving up without a fight?"

"You got any other ideas?"

"Sure. All we need to do is find eight other kids to be on the team."

"Right," I said, "and just whip them up into a winning team by Saturday."

I should have let the bat get me.

8

We could find only seven kids who were stupid enough to play against the Bombers. They were all second-graders. It was the first time any of them had been asked to be on a team.

Only one kid, Randy, had ever seen a soccer ball. He turned out to be a dynamite goalie. The rest of them were a disaster. Wendell was pretty fast, but his glasses kept slipping down over his nose and he ran into people. Francine was trying to get her bird-watching badge for

Brownies. Every time a bird flew overhead, she'd stop playing to watch it. Then she had to write its name down in her notebook. That's usually when Wendell would run into her. Hector was great at running, but he'd get his games mixed up and dodge the ball instead of kicking it. Dodgeball was the big sport in second grade.

Angel and I practiced together when the others weren't there. She filled me in on the rules of the game. I was getting pretty good, but the little kids couldn't learn fast enough.

By Thursday night, I knew we were in real trouble. "It's hopeless," I said, after the other kids had gone home.

"Maybe not," Angel said. "You and I work well together, and Randy's great in the goal. Sometimes that's enough to carry a whole team."

She showed me a few new moves. We practiced for a while as the sun was going down.

"You're not bad," she said, "but watch out

for that shoelace." Then she slipped the ball away from me before I even saw her foot.

"How did you do that?"

Angel grinned. "I took your mind off the game for a second. It works every time."

"Would it work on the Bombers? If the other kids could take their minds off the game, you and I could make the goals."

"Maybe. Let's watch the Bombers practice. We can pick out their weak spots."

We hid in the bushes Friday afternoon and watched the Bombers play. Angel took notes:

Steve — chews gum
Jessie — always scratching
Moose — combs hair a lot

We stayed just long enough to get what we needed. Then we slipped away without being seen. We were ready to launch Operation Bust-the-Bombers.

9

We were feeling great until we got to the playing field the next day. The Bombers fell all over each other laughing when they saw our team. "You guys need a name?" Steve asked. "How about 'The Nerd, the Frizz, and the Seven Dwarfs'?"

It looked as if every kid in the school was there to watch. The Bombers must have sold tickets.

We gathered the team in a huddle. "Okay,"

Angel said. "Do you all understand what you're supposed to do? Francine, quit checking out that robin and pay attention."

"I know, I know," Francine said, sticking her notebook back in her pocket. "I'm in charge of getting Steve."

"That's right," I said. "Hector, you've got Moose, and Jessie belongs to Wendell. Remember, when you see Angel or me wink, you go into action."

The whole first half was a disaster. Angel and I winked every time we got the ball, but nothing happened. Francine was more interested in the birds than she was in Steve. Hector was afraid to get near Moose, and Wendell kept forgetting what he was supposed to do. The Bombers were ahead one to nothing at halftime. If Randy hadn't blocked so many goals, it would have been about twenty to nothing.

It was time for a pep talk. "Do you want to go into third grade next year as nerds or as the team that busted the Bayside Bombers?" I said.

"I just want to live to be old enough for third grade," Hector said.

Wendell cleaned the mud off his glasses. "Me, too."

Suddenly Francine yelled, "Not me! I wanna be a Bomber Buster!" Pretty soon they were all jumping up and down, chanting "Bomber Busters! Bomber Busters!"

The team had changed. I could feel it. Francine punched me in the arm as we went back out on the field. "Go, Busters!" she yelled, not even glancing at a whole flock of swallows that flew overhead.

The Busters ran all over the field, charging any Bomber who got the ball. They didn't understand the game, but at least they had the Bombers confused.

Angel got the ball and started dribbling it down the field. Moose went after her, and she passed it to me. When I got to the goal, Steve was ready for me. But Francine was ready for Steve. "Want a piece of gum?" she asked.

Steve looked away just long enough for me to slip the ball into the goal.

"One to one!" Angel yelled. "Tie score!"

We went back to the center line and Jessie kicked off. Then I got the ball and winked. Jessie was right in front of me, but Wendell ran up to her. "Hey, Jessie," he said, "that looks like poison ivy on your arm." Jessie didn't try to stop me as I ducked around her. She was too busy scratching.

Moose came at me. I winked at Hector. By the time I passed Moose, he was combing his hair and saying, "Does it look okay now?"

Our troubles weren't over. Steve was watching every move I made. Francine tried, but Steve wouldn't fall for the gum trick twice. I saw an opening and passed to Angel. Then Steve blocked her, too.

It looked as if our tricks — and luck — had run out.

10

Just then I heard Wendell yell, "Hey, Steve. Your fly is open!"

Steve clutched his shorts, and the ball sailed past him into the goal. The buzzer went off.

"We won!" Angel screamed, grabbing me. "I told you we could do it."

The Busters crowded around us, jumping up and down. As I looked over their heads, I saw Jessie give Wendell a shove. "Oh-oh. Looks like Wendell needs our help." We all ran over.

"Whaddaya mean, poison ivy?" Jessie yelled. "There's nothing on my arm." That didn't stop her from scratching.

Wendell pushed his glasses back on his nose. "Looked like it to me. I guess I need a new prescription."

Jessie pushed him again. "Dumb little kid. How can you play soccer, if you can't even see straight?"

Wendell grinned. "We won, didn't we?"

"You were just lucky," Jessie said, and stormed off.

"Here comes trouble," Angel whispered. Steve was heading our way.

"I want to know who said my fly was open," Steve demanded. "These shorts don't even have a fly. That was a rotten trick."

"I . . . uh. . . ." I was stalling for time until Angel said something. She didn't.

Then a little hand held out a pack of gum. "Want some?" Francine asked. "You can have the thing."

"Oh . . . thanks," Steve said, snatching the pack from her.

We just stood there for a minute while Steve chewed, staring at us. "You two are pretty good," he said, finally. "Your goalie's not bad, either, but he's too young. You want to be Bombers?"

"I'm from Indiana," Angel said. "I have to go back home at the end of the month."

Steve turned to me. "How about you, Brian? You can dump the dwarfs and join up with us."

I couldn't believe it. Steve Grebe was really asking me to be a Bayside Bomber. I didn't need to blackmail him this time. He was asking me because I was a good player.

I was all set to say yes, when I turned and looked at the Busters. They were huddled together, watching us. Francine's lower lip was starting to tremble. Then I remembered. Without those kids, I'd be hiding my face from the whole school about now.

I took one last look at the Bombers passing the ball back and forth across the field. They really were the best team in the whole town.

"Thanks anyway, Steve," I said. "But I'm sticking with the Bomber Busters. We have a big season ahead of us."